This book belongs to:

- - - - - - - - - - - - - - -

to Laetitia

Musgrove and the Easter Eggs

by Ilona Rodgers

Stacey International

Hermione and Musgrove were making a cake for Easter.

"I hope it is going to be as good as the cake my Aunt Aurelia used to make," said Musgrove adding an extra handful of raisins.

"By the way," he went on, "tomorrow is Easter Day, so we need to paint some hard-boiled eggs."

"We don't need to,"
said Hermione. "We've
already got chocolate eggs!"
She ran out of the kitchen
and returned with a wooden
bowl full of Easter chocolates.
"Chocolate eggs won't do,"
insisted Musgrove. "We need
proper eggs."

Musgrove put on his bowler hat, and off they set to the Fresh and Wild shop on Westbourne Grove. There they bought half-a-dozen, very organic, freshly-laid eggs in an Easter basket.

Back home, Hermione settled at her table, opened her new box of watercolours, and straight away she began to paint.

"This egg will be like Papa's suit — dark blue with stripes."

"This egg will be like Papa's special tie — bright red with blue dots."

"This egg will be like
Papa's Tuesday shirt —
light blue with stripes."

"This egg will be like
Mama's new scarf - orange
with snowflakes."

"This egg will be like Mama's favourite dress, the one she wears out to dinner — green with pink spots."

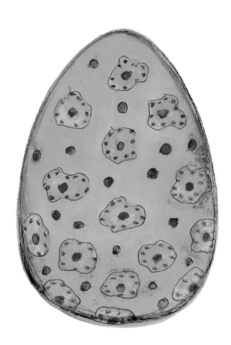

"And the last egg will be like Mama's party shoes, because no other Mama has such lovely shoes — lilac with golden bows."

When the eggs were dry, Hermione brought them into the kitchen and put them back in the Easter basket. How pretty they looked!

Next day was Easter Day.
In the morning, Hermione
and Musgrove were woken
by a strange sound. It
was a kind of chattering-
pattering sound.
Where was it coming from?
The drawing room?
The bathroom?
Or was it the kitchen?

Up jumped Musgrove and Hermione. They hurried into the kitchen.

In the Easter basket, among lots of broken egg shells, sat six chattering-pattering chicks.

One was dark blue with stripes.

Another one was bright
red with blue dots.

The third was light
blue with stripes.

The fourth was orange
with snowflakes.

The fifth was green with
pink spots.

The sixth was lilac
with golden bows.

When the chicks saw Musgrove they flapped their tiny wings, scrambled out of their basket and chirping cheerfully ran up to Musgrove.

"They think you are their mama", laughed Hermione, and hid behind his hairy back.

Musgrove threw up his arms, and down fell all his newspapers. "My eggs! My eggs!" he cried. "Oh dear me! We forgot to boil them!"

Happy Easter !

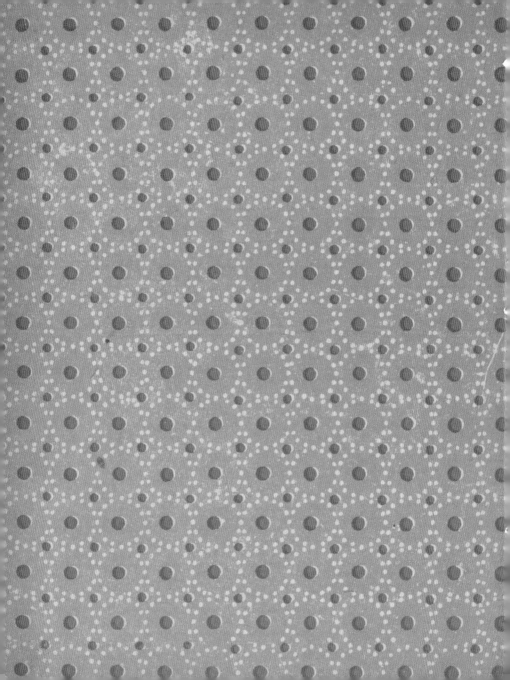